Fred the Frog
Finds A Friend

Written & Illustrated by:
Courtney M Jones

copyright 2013 Courtney M Jones   All Rights Reserved

Fred is a sweet little frog

2

who likes to hop from rock to rock.

4

Even though he wears a smile

Fred feels really sad.

"If only I could make a friend,"
Fred said.

"Then I could feel happy again."

Fred hopped toward some thick,

tall grass

8

and leaped to the other side.

10

"Why, what a pretty and peaceful pond!" said Fred.

"Maybe there's food I can try to find!"

12

His little tummy was growling.

Poor Fred has been hungry for days.

14

Just then a group of flies

went buzzing by

and landed on the lily pads.

"Why, what yummy yummy flies!" Fred cried.

"I must jump into the pond to catch them!"

18

Suddenly a big orange fish popped up out of the water and swam towards little Fred.

"What are you doing here?" The fish asked with a growl.

"Don't you know that I live here?"

20

"I'm very sorry Mr. Fish." said little Fred.

"But I am very very hungry and there are flies on the lily pad I must catch."

The big orange fish sneered at little Fred.
"I don't think so." said the fish.
"If your toes touch this water I will eat you up!"

Just then a tiny little beetle appeared from underneath a lily pad.

"Now listen here fish!" said the tiny beetle.

"This frog must eat his meal! What if you were very hungry and were not allowed to eat? How would you feel?"

24

The big orange fish took a moment to think about what the beetle said. "I think I would be hungry and sad just like this little frog." said the fish.

The big orange fish had an idea!

"You may pass but your toes must stay on the lily pads. I will not eat you if you agree."

Fred was very very happy!

"Thank you Mr. Fish!" said little Fred.

"I promise to stay on the lily pads!"

"You heard the little frog!" said the tiny beetle. "Now shoo shoo away from here!" he said to the fish while waving his itty bitty arms.

With a flip of his big fins and a loud SPLASH the fish swam away.

The tiny beetle watched with joy as little Fred hopped happily from lily pad to lily pad and ate his meal.

Fred was very happy to have a full tummy.

"Thank you so much Mr. beetle."

said little Fred.

"You saved my life today."

"You are very welcome."

said the tiny beetle.

"I have been hungry

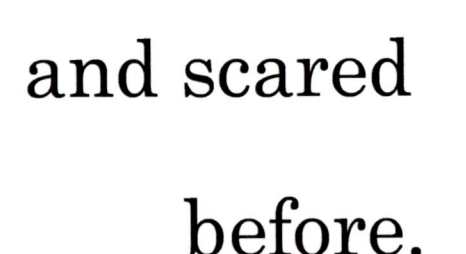

and scared

before.

I wanted to help because I would hope that someone would help me too."

Little Fred felt much better now because the tiny beetle had empathy for him.

Empathy means understanding how someone else is feeling.

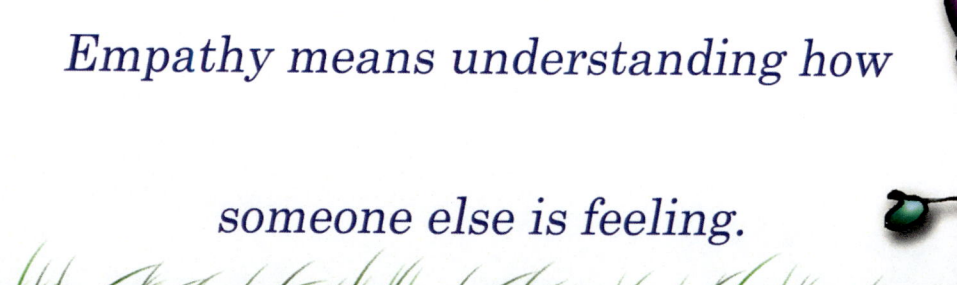

"I am so happy that we found each other." said little Fred. "Would you like to be my friend?"

"Of course I will be your friend!"

said the tiny beetle.

"Best friends forever!"

Also by Children's Book Author & Illustrator Courtney M Jones:

In A Room You Will Find series:

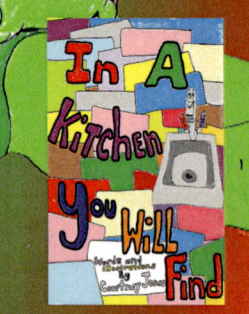

In A
Kitchen
You Will Find

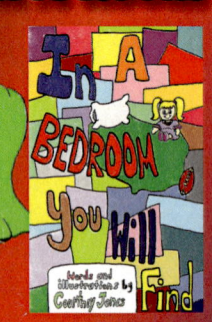

In A
Bedroom
You Will Find

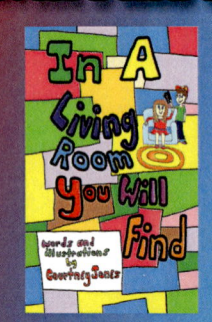

In A
Living Room
You Will Find

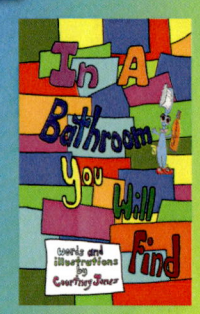

In A
Bathroom
You Will Find

visit
courtneymjones.com
to purchase and learn more about Courtney's
books and to print free coloring and activity sheets featuring the characters from Courtney's Books!

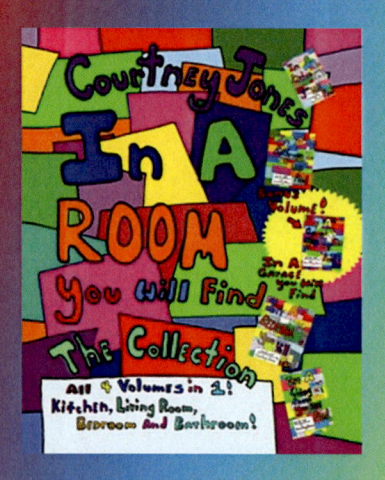

Or own the entire series in one Fun Filled booK! Courtney Jones In A Room You Will Find; The Collection features all 4 of the In A Room You Will Find series and also includes a BONUS volume, never before released: In A Garage You Will Find, only available in this Collection!

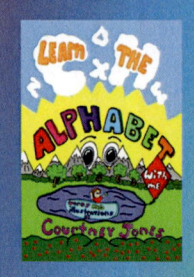

Also by Courtney M Jones:
Learn the Aplhabet With Me
Bold, Bright colos and silly rhymes will have your child learning their letters in no time!

A Free Bookmark

Just For You!

Write your name

on the line and carefully

cut along the dotted line.

Have fun reading!

visit **courtneymjones.com**
for free coloring & activity sheets
on the Kids Corner Page of Courtney's website!

My Name is:

_____

&
Fred says

"Reading is
Ribbit
Fun!"

I AGREE!

Made in the USA
Middletown, DE
21 March 2017